Puck My Prey

a stalker hockey dark romance

Jericho Chimers

Sofia Aves

The only rules that matter to me are on the ice, and the ones I make for her.
Even when she doesn't know we're playing.

Cora Grace has a reputation as a b*ll buster. She's who the club calls in when a media sh*tstorm hits, the one they rely on to keep us in line when the players don't play nice.

Cora thinks she can tame us. Thinks she can tame *me*. She has her own set of games where there's only one winner:

Her.

What she doesn't know yet is that we're already playing a game, and I don't play by her rules.

But she'll know soon enough.

First Edition

EBOOK ISBN 978-1-923471-15-3

PRINT ISBN 978-1-923471-16-0

CONTENT WARNING

The Jericho Chimeras don't play nice off the ice. Don't ask me why. Coach refuses to talk to me right now and there's a weird shaped mascot driving the charter bus. Each of the boys have their kink but their stories are also steeped in trauma and scars. This book contains several dark themes. Please read through the list and choose your reading Chimera wisely.

- Biting
- Assault
- Stalking
- Voyeurism

- Exhibitionism
- Spying
- Predator/prey play
- Dominance
- Submission
- Brattiness
- Past trauma
- Estrangement
- Feeding
- Praise play
- Peeping
- Obsession

Please be safe in your reading habits. This book may not be safe for all readers. If you'd still love to read one of my books, but this one isn't for you, I'd love to have you. SHE'S A HOT CHRISTMAS MESS is a fun (and safe) place to start.

Enjoy your Chimera. In a dark place is best.

. . .

Sweet dreams,

Sofia xx

for Elizabeth

CHAPTER ONE

HEATH

"Not a single one of you deserve to wear the Jericho Chimera jersey after last night's debacle."

Ballbuster extraordinaire Cora Brooks stood at the player's bench halfway through practice after a truly shitty morning and laid down the law on her first day back at the Chimeras after a hiatus since our last major fuck up.

Or maybe she thought she did.

Half of my teammates ogled her thoughtfully. The other half were probably still drunk after last night's clusterfuck. Not that I blamed them.

Cap stood with his arms crossed, gripping his

stick like he wanted to ram it down her throat, sending subliminal messages to Coach who stood slightly behind the curvy goddess in the power suit who should never have been anywhere near the ice.

And me?

I watched the woman the club called to intervene when the media storm grew too hot. I knew why. It was either they called her in to fix the mess that we didn't, or someone—likely several someones —got sacked.

And that wasn't happening on my watch. Not after last night.

Cora paced the player's bench like it was her own personal sand box. She had no idea she was so far out of her depth, but it would be fun to watch her flounder. We weren't like any version of the team that she'd attempted to manage before, nor were we the regular misfit players.

"This room is full of grown men who behave like toddlers. Every one of your faces are all over mainstream media rags after last night, and a few minor channels. Not one of you," —she glared at every face who dared snicker at her outburst. Exactly who was the toddler here?— "Will be playing on the weekend if we don't fix this by Thursday. That gives you," — she made a second fake ass show of checking her fancy watch— "exactly five days to get your house-keeping in order. Be squeaky clean. Apologies all round. Fix that poor woman's reputation *and each of your own* or you will not have a fucking job come Friday. Am I clear?"

The resounding silence that boomed across the ice crackled with its failure to answer her.

If this woman expected any of us to bounce back with a chorus of *'yes, ma'ams'*, she was shit out of luck.

Hell, she'd just threatened the best thing anyone of us had worked for—and we *had* each worked our asses off for the positions we held on the team—that took us years to get here. What reaction did she expect?

Beside me, Shannon Incarson reached back and scratched his ass. "So, we're good to keep training, then?" he asked politely.

I smirked. He couldn't have given a better *fuck you* to the little lady in the power pants suit the color of pristine ice that settled over the luscious curves and glimpses of honey tanned skin. Skin I'd love to see more of, though under different conditions, maybe. See how she took to submission and what relinquishing control over doling it out looked like on her.

That was always my favorite game, had been for years. Working out which of the women who loved to cling tightest to their control out of pure desperation would be the hardest to give it up but the most fucking stunning when they did.

Cora Brooks, with her severe bun, white blonde hair tightly tucked back behind her ears in a perfect knot, glaring at us through black rimmed glasses, her make up perfect...She was my top candidate for the sort of woman who would never want to relinquish control.

No more than I'd ever give up my position on the Jericho Chimeras team. That took me four years to earn, training every damn day just to get myself noticed by scouts all the way through high school.

The woman before me would be the perfect submissive, and she'd fight every inch of the way. It would be hell, and she would be beautiful.

Huh. Pity that would never happen. Pity she was here to fuck with my team. We could have had so much fun.

Before Shannon could open his smart ass mouth and say something else to piss her off, I broke rank, skating backwards. Cora's eyes locked onto me. Her pretty little mouth opened—to rip me a new one, call me off the ice, I didn't much care—but it was Coach who called me back.

"Valentine. Rein it in." Unlike her temper tantrum before, his voice whiplashed across the ice, catching me at chest height.

I let my stick dance with the puck a moment longer, and took a clean, unobstructed shot at the goal.

A blind shot, because the goal was behind me, and I kept my eyes locked on her the entire time as it sailed neatly into the net. The score ticked over on the board in my periphery.

"Yes, sir." I kept my tone respectful, and finally flicked my gaze to Coach.

His eyes narrowed at my show ponying. I'd pay for that little stunt later. "Stay on the ice. I got a few words for you. Hux, you too, son. The rest of you, follow Miss Brooks into the main office for a full debriefing on your media habits for this week. It'll be a change up and I expect you to treat her like you treat me."

A second round of silence whispered across the ice, its significance lost on the stranger in our midst.

Cap knew better than to open his mouth, though my lips curled up in a derisive smile as the team followed Miss Cora Brooks off the ice.

I waited until she was the last of the line filing away from the bench, and spoke to her poker straight back.

The ones in control are always the ones with the most scars on the inside.

Hell, I couldn't wait to discover hers. We were playing a game, even if she didn't know we'd started yet.

"Enjoy your podium, Miss Brooks," I murmured to the emptying stadium.

Ward Bishop, the Chimera's coach, muttered curses to the ice as he took up position behind me, no doubt ready to rip me a new one the moment her perfectly curved tush vacated the ice. The one person who shouldn't be there who I aimed my comments directly at offered me no reaction whatsoever.

Yep, Cora Brooks reined in that control so tight I was surprised she didn't snap on the spot. Maybe that was why she had a hissy fit the moment she stepped up earlier. Or maybe her little tantrum had nothing to do with my team's apparent shenanigans whatsoever.

Damn, we were gonna have so much fun together.

I wondered which one of us would break first,

and if she'd enjoy kneeling for me...

Or if I would be the one on my knees for her.

"Wake up, Valentine," Coach snapped as he skated circles around Cap and me a dozen breaths later once we were sure that we were alone on the ice once more. "If the two of you don't pull your heads out of your asses, it will be your jobs that Cora Brooks calls for first. You, because it's your responsibility to talk sense into the assholes who just followed her with their tails tucked—" Coach glared at Hux like the star of our team was Cap's personal fault. "And you—" His slate gray glare landed on me, "—You, since Hux was home in bed with his woman, *you*, Valentine, are going to tell me what in the hell happened with that woman last night that has the media with their panties in a twist. Because, what, you all wanted to dabble in a little group sex? Indulged in a party night before four a.m. training? Those rags are all full of shit and we both know it. I don't need to read the cheap tabloid she brought in to know that. And I *know* that, because you wouldn't let them do anything half as stupid on your watch, would you? Right?" His voice cracked around the empty rink, tinged with the faintest edge of desperation.

Coach got right up in my face, which was saying something for a man at least fifteen years older than me and nearly a foot shorter, though Ward Bishop was no slouch. I was just a big, Black giant, which was why, while Solace Hunter was off with an injury from two games back, Coach put me in as stand in goalie.

Apparently, that position came with a side service for team protectors. The trust he threw at them was made for damn broad shoulders. Solace wore that mantle just fine, but those were some big skates to fill.

I stared at Coach down, and refused to flinch.

"No, I won't let them flounder on my watch," I said quietly, my arms folded across my chest.

"Good. I didn't fucking think so," the man before me huffed, though he deflated somewhat when I didn't arc up at him as he obviously expected.

"Then what the hell *happened?*" Hux glided across the ice to pick up the collection of papers Cora left behind. "This doesn't say much apart from the fact that half the team was drunk last night." He shot me a pointed look.

"Yeah, they got drunk," I acknowledged. "It was

meant to be Solace's buck's party, remember? He was getting married, and then the knee injury took him out." I shrugged, because let's face it—without that injury I'd probably still be warming myself a place on the Reserve squad bench with the rest of the hopefuls.

"And what, they couldn't wait for a few more nights, or his actual event?" Coach looked disgusted.

Even though I agreed with the sentiment, I kept my face carefully blank. Hux watched me thoughtfully from a distance, tapping the tabloids against his thigh.

"Maybe not," I finally conceded.

The coach blew out a breath through whitened lips. "Is that all I'm going to get from the pair of you?"

Silence met his question.

Closing ranks on the man who handpicked me from utter obscurity and the *nobody who's nobody* list of the year might not be my smartest choice. Last night we made a decision as a team. I refused to be the one to not meet that mark two weeks into playing for my dream squad.

The coach exhaled a long breath slowly. "Fine, Valentine. You heard the lady. Don't give her a reason to name you on her shit list. And you'd better have answers for her when she pulls you into my damn office later today. Because she will."

"For answers or because she's taken up residence in your office?" I kept my voice low, but we all heard the question that I didn't bother to hide.

Coach skated away from me, the tension in his shoulders telling its own story.

I mentally added his weight to my protector's list. What was the point in shouldering the team weight if I couldn't return the favor for the man who lifted me out of development squad hell? The man gave up authority over the team, albeit grudgingly, for the next few days, as well as his office.

Maybe it was time that I went and saw Miss Cora Brooks ahead of schedule. Just to see if I could help out the woman I fully intended to torment a little before I broke her.

I hoped Coach wasn't too attached to his desk.

CHAPTER TWO

CORA

I crossed another name off my list, swallowing a groan along with a cold mouthful of black tea. The coffee in the player's lounge didn't bear looking at. A few coffee bags one of the girls seemed to favor smelled stale. She presented me with a cup paired with a huge smile and a slice of heavily laden avocado toast that I nearly wore when she tripped toward me. I declined, unsure if she intended the move as a prank, or was just inherently clumsy.

Not that I blamed her. She seemed sweet enough, after all. People were the main reason I avoided the main club office. There sufficient testosterone in the Jericho Chimera's home to fuel several Friday Night Fights, but that wasn't why I was groaning.

The next name on my interview list for today was Heath 'Cupid' Valentine.

No bonus points for guessing how he earned his nickname.

But the reason I groaned was because of all the players I'd seen today, not only was Heath Valentine the last on my list, meaning I was exhausted after dealing with the closed ranks and bullshit behavior of the rest of the team, he was also the only one who actually got under my skin.

Because for some reason, I *let him* work his way under my skin with that little stunt he pulled earlier on the ice this morning. I'd felt tiny. And he'd been indifferent, almost. That pissed me off. More than his team mate, Shannon, speaking out of turn, which was the sort of behavior I'd expected from a group of drunken loud mouths who had half assaulted a woman the night before, though not one of them had confirmed the action yet.

And neither had she.

Hence the closing of ranks.

And the only evidence the world had of any of it was of Heath Valentine with his jacket held over the woman's head to conceal her face while he walked her to his car the night before trying to hide her torn dress and the bite marks on her ruined skin. That image was splashed across the face of the world and I could take that back no matter what I did. The action still didn't disguise the bruises and bite marks evident all over her body that the media shitstorm ate up declaring the Chimeras displaying their true nature, each taking on a different beastly form as they ripped the poor soul apart.

Thankfully, she hadn't pressed charges—yet—and the team weren't talking. Both of that meant exactly zero police engagement, but media being media meant, police charges or no, I had a helluva job this morning in damage control. The least of which was finding out what the fuck actually happened.

Maybe I should have started with him in the first place.

And then Heath Valentine ignored me during morning chit chat time, setting the standard for the rest of his team. Hux didn't step in, not that I expected the Chimeras captain to do anything, though the show of support would have been decent, but Coach backed me. I appreciated that, being the outsider. Since all that happened first thing this morning back on the ice where I knew I should never have tried to address the team en masse in the first damn place, the rest of my day went to shit and back fast as fuck. No amount of premium grade, if stale, caffeine from their coffeemaker could fix that.

Maybe I should have taken up the offer of avocado toast after all.

The club called me in when they needed a mess fixed that they couldn't cleanup for themselves. The last time I entered this office outside of professional functions and PR sessions was when two players were fired over the sort of drugs scandal that stuck. That was during the reign of the captain before Hux. The Chimeras had been reasonably clean ever since.

But then, Hux hadn't been there last night, and neither was his best friend, Solace.

And look what happened with their stand-in protector.

It wasn't like *goalie* was synonymous with *defender* off the ice for the Jericho Chimeras, but Solace damn well made sure for the past few years that the team stayed in line whenever they weren't playing a game. His being out hurt the team in more ways than one, I knew, and they were some pretty big skates to fill.

Each of the players had their own personality

both on and off the ice and some of those lined up with their positions. Others were a little bit...

Extra.

I wasn't sure about Heath Valentine just yet. No one was. New blood always changed the team dynamic. Last night's epic failure spoke to just that.

I shuffled papers across my borrowed desk, seething at the fact that I hadn't even made it to addressing my growing list of emails from both the board of directors and media contacts with whom I had currently maintained radio silence. But that wouldn't last forever.

The moment any of the players stepped out into the parking lot outside the club, they were fair game for the media shit storm that circled like a threatening tornado. Whether the girl was a willing participant in last night's orgy, the boys decided they were aiming for a polyamorous relationship, or I needed to reset my opinion of the players who had earned my respect over the years, I honestly had no idea how I was going to salvage the club's reputation of the cluster fuck of epic proportions without jeopardizing the team's reputation and jobs.

Hux, Coach... sure, I could protect them—probably. But at this point, and without anybody else talking to me, I doubted even that. It wasn't like I had any other choice. I'd given the boys a five day deadline that was fast becoming four. The reality was that if I didn't have the information that I needed by the end of the day, my timeline was likely cut short to tomorrow. Heads would roll fast. Media response was required and I needed to speak to the female question.

Because they sure as fuck couldn't.

The papers that I shuffled in my hands crumpled and tore.

"Fuck, fuck, *fuck*." I kicked Coach's desk and stubbed my toe. *"Fuck."* I added the extra for emphasis.

"It never did anything to you," a deep voice berated me gently.

My teeth clicked against each other as pain and iron bloomed across the back of my tongue. "Fuck." That came out muffled and slightly high-pitched. "Ow." I nursed my bitten tongue.

I glared balefully at where Heath Valentine lounged against Coach's door frame. His bulk, that should be in no way different to any of the other players but way anyway in sheer presence, filled it. But Valentine didn't just fill the doorway. He obliterated the space that any regular person would have taken up. The man was enormous. No wonder they picked him to sub in for Solace while he was off injured.

Perhaps he was more like solace than I thought.

I held the gaze of the man who would be lucky if he would survive tonight to be in the office tomorrow at this rate.

"You're early," I accused him.

Both eyebrows raised over dark skin. A shadow crossed his gaze as he watched me. "And you're surprised. Why are you surprised, Miss Cora Brooks?" My name rolled from his tongue like honeyed tea.

I hated the way he said it. Like he'd taken possession of me, somehow.

"Let me make this clear. Once," I snapped. More blood filled my mouth. I swallowed the unwelcome tang back. "I'll let you know when I'm ready for you, and then you come running, especially after the way the team has behaved today, thanks to your... Behavior this morning," I held his imposing gaze despite feeling as though I was less than half his height and held my ground. "You'll tell me everything I need to know. Is that–"

"Absolutely," he said softly.

Respectfully.

I blinked.

What just happened?

"Fine. I'll call you in ten minutes," I huff.

Valentine inclined his head and ducked out of the doorway. Despite his bulk and height that must be near seven feet—exaggeration, six and a half, he just looked huge to tiny duck butt me. For the life of me I couldn't recall his exact stats that earlier this morning I could have rattled off like a well-trained parrot—his footfalls as he disappeared along the hallway were near silent.

Like a hunter.

My fingers curled into fists at my sides. Damn that man and his ability to influence both my own reactions and the team for the short period of time he had been around. My teeth weren't the only things that clacked as I turned back to my paperwork and continued shredding the top page into confetti.

Fuck Valentine and his mind games. Fuck him and his manners.

Fuck this club and fuck this day.

All I wanted was to go home, bury my head in a pillow and scream into the void like a toddler. But I couldn't do that, because I was an adult—some of the time—and I had a job to do.

I inhaled water and read through my scanned notes, attempting to formulate a plan from the information I'd gathered for the rest of the day. My phone rang on my desk.

"Yes?"

I'd never made a habit of answering with my name. If someone didn't know who they were calling, they shouldn't be calling.

"Cora! How's your morning going!" A chipper, thin voice bitch slapped me from the other end.

I bit back a groan. "Uh, just dandy, Peatie. Whatcha got for me this morning?"

"Well, after your Chimeras ate up the landscape last night, there's not a lot more going on, but rumor has it..."

I closed my eyes and zoned out.

Rumor has it was Peatie's favorite line. Over a year ago, Peatie had pulled my number from the Chimera's business directory and decided he, as a mini media PR mogul, would 'assist' me by providing daily updates. Usually, his information was actually helpful. I stayed off social media unless I needed it, and he was fairly reliable with his sources of comings and goings in the sports world, major shifts, scandals, etc., etc., etc. Even if we weren't friends, I did appreciate the work he put in.

I nodded a lot, put in a few well placed *'yeps'* and hung up without wasting too much time.

Twenty minutes later, my mind was as blank as it had been before Valentine appeared in the office doorway. I glanced at my phone and made a call that I hated. Asking for help had never been my strong point, but right now I didn't see your way around it.

> CORA: Best approach for Valentine?

> COACH: Straight up. You'll earn his respect fastest for that.

> CORA: Even after this morning?

I felt pitiful, begging for validation.

> COACH: Test the waters. Valentine's not a shit stirrer. He's a protector. But if you threaten the team, he'll come straight for you.

> CORA: Great. Thanks.

I read over the text messages once more and straightened. *Time to face the music.* I'd made him wait long enough.

"Valentine," I called in a clear voice.

Dammit, I should've gone to the kitchen and

made another stale coffee. Or tea. Or matcha, even. Anything that contained caffeine would've been worth it. I poked my head out of the office and nearly ran straight into a Chimera jersey-wearing chest. Had he been waiting right outside the doorway? It was a damn good thing I didn't recite my notes out loud, selling state secrets to the nearest bidder for free. I found myself nose-to-recyclable-takeaway-cup he presented me with.

"What's this?"

"I wasn't sure if you ate today. We can be a handful."

I blinked at the group pronoun usage. Not *I*, but *we*. My head canted one side as I repeated his phrase and threw his words back at him, reversing their meaning. "Have *you* eaten today?" I ushered him into the office, watching carefully as he placed the tall takeaway cup onto my desk alongside a brown paper bag. "Should I be checking for a bomb?"

Valentine was careful with his motions and I cursed myself for my positioning in not being able to see his face when he responded. "Yes. No."

I closed my mouth, closed the door, and waited for more.

My captive Chimera stood with his back to me. Perhaps our waiting game was a two sided coin.

Unable to stand still and yet craving to see his expression, I circled around him, giving the huge man as wide a berth as Coach's small office allowed.

I found it interesting that Coach could've asked for a much larger office in this building, but didn't. My own office in the adjacent building was double the size but we had decided that the interviews needed to be here today. I made a mental note to ask if he could be moved later for more space since he well and truly earned it putting up with the players like the one tormenting me now.

"No?"

"Coffee. Lunch. It's there for you."

I nodded. Valentine still didn't move as I finished my circle. "And have you?"

When he didn't answer, I looked up and discovered the office was so much smaller than I expected. Because Heath was *right fucking* there. I slid the food and coffee across the desk, sat my ass down, and scooted Coach's thread bare chair that was most definitely not leather several feet back to garner myself breathing room.

"Why does Coach have his office here? The smallest office here," I murmured, then cursed myself for bothering. That was a question for either Hux or Solace who had been around the team for years, rather than a man who joined the Chimeras full ranks weeks ago and wouldn't be here by week's end.

Heath Valentine stared at me with unreadable black eyes. That same shadow as before flickered across his unfathomable gaze before it disappeared as fast as it came on. Unblinking, unyielding. This man was as hard as fuck and the only way I would get in would be if he would let me.

Don't threaten the team.

Ward Bishop's advice was solid. As coach, he held responsibility over the team, but unfortunately, the rest of the Chimeras hadn't left me much of an option. Everything rode on what Valentine said to me in the next twenty minutes.

"He wants to be close to the ice. To the team. Here for what we need." Valentine returned my study, though his stance remained relaxed.

I raised both eyebrows ,mimicking his behavior from before. "Are you also a mind reader?"

The faint smile from before lifted Valentine's plush arched lips. "I asked him the same question on my first day."

"Why?"

His smile remained." Because I expected all executives—which Coach definitely isn't—to work in a gold gilt office. To a poor kid from a shit neighborhood this place looks like a palace. But—" He watched me carefully, "—you know that."

I did know that.

"Did you say anything else?" I forestalled his next question. Valentine never blinked at my interruption. I offered an olive branch. "I don't want anyone off the team. It's my job to be a barrier here too." *Even if I don't wear a jersey.*

"He told me to take care of the team in Solace's absence."

"Is that why you took the traumatized girl to your car?"

"Yes." The images of Valentine were burned into my mind, but I glanced down at the black and white photo anyway, just to check. See if I was wrong, but I knew I wasn't. Even grainy the image was clear, but with height, his shoulders were recognizable beneath a taut black shirt as he held a leather jacket across her tiny frame.

"Do you know who did this?" I pushed the tabloid on top of the pile across the desk to him.

"Yes."

Alright. It was a one word answer, but we were getting somewhere. Because that *yes* was more than anyone else had given me all day.

I blew out a shallow breath. My heart began to

pound. If this was my crux point, I had no idea how to approach it. Maybe Valentine was right. I was exhausted, after all. A ten minute nap would relife my batteries. My vision blurred. I shook my head, attempting to focus.

Valentine still watched me carefully, his breath slowing. "You should eat something."

My hands drifted towards the brown paper bag without my permission. I snatched them back. "Let's finish this first."

Wait, did I just give him a concession? Did I actually just agree to do what he said? This man was bad for me. He needed to get out of the office as soon as he could. But first I needed to finish this.

"Will you tell me who?" Shit. That was a close ended question. *I'm better than this.*

"No." His enigmatic smile was back again.

Damnit. I earned that. I offered him a faint smile of my own. That one was on me.

"Fair enough." I gestured to the seat opposite my borrowed desk, unsurprised when he didn't move or acknowledge me in any way.

No one had used that seat all day.

It was time for a different approach. "Did you get your jacket back?"

I knew he didn't. It was hanging in the cupboard Coach's tiny bathroom off the side of the office.

At least he didn't use the communal one.

Though the state of his desk chair *did* match the size of his office en suite. I knew what I was getting Coach for Christmas.

That was, assuming we all still had jobs next week.

"Not yet," Valentine said softly, rolling his shoulders as though he missed the black leather that was splashed all over the front of every tabloid I picked up this morning.

I nodded. "Tell me about last night." I didn't make it a question. That one was open and he could take it as he liked. I needed to get his gauge fast.

My hands strayed towards the take away coffee. I picked it up without much thought, my palms sinking into its heat before my brain cussed me out for accepting his offering so freely.

"You need something, Cora, or you'll end up with a headache."

I ignored the pain already blooming behind my eyes for exactly that reason.

"Are you open to a role as my conscience? Last night," I reminded him as I cradled the coffee and took a sip.

Pure black coffee, no sugar, no cream. The syrupy liquid slipped down my throat. My eyes shuttered and I swore I could count the shots in that steaming cup.

Hot enough to burn, but not scald. Only one place made coffee that perfect. Pity that I never made it halfway across town on my lunch break or before work to get there.

My eyes snapped open as the implications hit me. "That coffee shop is twenty minutes away. Did you drive out to get this?" Indignation burned the back of my throat, turning sweet syrup to bitter dregs.

His enigmatic smile returned. "I can jog."

That. Boy.

Puck me over, these chimeras were going to kill me.

I clutched my coffee to my chest. That drink was *mine* and I refused to give it up, even if it meant handing over concessions to a Chimera I didn't trust this early in.

"Did you ask someone?" My brain whirred, trying to work out who spilled the literal beans on my preferences.

Valentine watched me. "Her name is Corinne Weathers. I can provide her address. She was safe when I dropped her off at four a.m. No one on the team touched her, and none of them deserve to lose their jobs." His mouth shut and he tipped his head to one side. "That's all that you need to know, Cora. Eat. The headache will go away."

I stared at him. The cup rose in my hands and I took a deep sip, the action mesmerizing to both of us as his almost black eyes deepened impossibly.

"I'm glad you enjoy the coffee." And then Heath Cupid Valentine turned around and walked out of my temporary office like he had just been dismissed.

Only we weren't anywhere near done.

I clutched my coffee and tried not to pick at the brown paper bag as his perfectly formed tush left the office. *Gray sweats should be illegal.* I didn't have to look to know that the bag he had left me contained a cream cheese and lox toasted bagel.

My favorite.

CHAPTER THREE

HEATH

Five days to prove our innocence. That was the deadline Cora Brooks gave us. Four, really, by the time the team filed from the club's glassy black doors beneath the snarling chimera club logo emblazoned across the front of the building.

Or rather, where they didn't exit today.

The first time I walked through those doors, I wondered if it took someone a full time job keeping them clean. Now I knew the truth. Because apart from days like today, when the entire staff herded the team out through the back doors with their faces covered against the plethora of camera flashes like the bunch of criminals they weren't, no one came through those front doors or stood outside them.

No one cleaned them more than once a week.

The *pristine perfect* facade was just that.

A fucking lie.

Which was what drew me to Cora Brooks. The same thing that made me want to work for Coach. Why I circled the ice hour after hour, doing drills before everyone else arrived each morning and training in the club's custom built gym well after they left.

Because out here, where sweat rolled into every crevice and orifice my body possessed unchecked, I got a little bit dirty. A little bit filthy. Everything fucking ached. Muscles trembled as I neared the point of exhaustion, pushing both my body's physical and mental limits.

Punishing myself for not being there. Not being fast enough.

For not seeing what I should have that night.

And I'd do it all over again tomorrow.

But when I stepped outside into the darkened parking lot and thought I was the only one left to lock up, I found I'd made a mistake. Because Cora Brooks stood next to my bike, her eyes tracking over the matte black paintwork and back to me. Her body was encased in black head to toe; black tights that showed off every curve of her body, and there were plenty of those, a black crop, and black zip hoodie open at the front, leaving a tantalizing glimpse of bare skin at her stomach. Her feet pointed in one direction, her body in the other.

"Solace used to do that," she said finally, breaking the all-pervasive silence that hung in the darkness like a shadow between us that refused to budge as she invoked the name of the Chimera's prior goalie on hallowed club grounds.

"Stalk you?" I raised both eyebrows, wondering if the prior defender didn't need another busted kneecap.

She smirked, and fuck me if the way her lips curved didn't send blood rushing south to a different part of my anatomy. "I think he has a different female in mind for that. No," she cleared her throat. "Solace was always the last one out. Looks like you're sticking true to form for your position." Her voice dropped an octave, warbled a little.

Well fuck me if Cora Brooks actually gives a damn about the players she tortures.

After the way she attacked the rest of the team, I nearly didn't get her that damn coffee earlier, but I wanted to find out what her mouth felt like under mine more than I wanted to see her leave the building cussing and swearing. Besides, there were other ways to punish a woman for fucking with what was mine in all ways.

Other ways to make her *feel*.

But somehow, I didn't think that was her problem at all.

I rested my hand on the keypad, entering my code to lock up the building for the night without looking. "Good to know I make the mark." I held my breath when she opened her mouth to make some smart assed rebuttal, but nothing fell out. "Are you catching the bus home?" I knew she walked.

Cora ran her fingers along the lines of my bike, resting her blunt cut nails on the leather seat. "Thank you for the food today. I never make it to the coffee place." That last came out wistful.

I leaned my back against the harsh edge of the building, resisting the need to scratch my shoulder blades on it. "If it's what you want, you should make time."

Her eyes narrowed. "Are you telling me how to organize my day, Chimera boy?"

I watched her, letting my expression settle into something more neutral than interested and prayed she wouldn't look down, otherwise we'd be having a whole other conversation. "You should run. Now."

"There you go, telling me what to do again." She huffed, and inched toward. "Why the hell do you think you can tell me what I can do, where I can go?"

Why aren't you running?

Telling her where she could go hadn't been the point, but I didn't correct that misconception just yet.

"I'll follow you, make sure you get home alright. It's been hectic." More than hectic.

A ground level office window bore a distinct crack that hadn't been there this morning. I suspected one of the media crew had attempted to gain access to the building while we were in a meeting earlier and gotten stuck. That mob level violence was a terrifying thing. Media weren't my favorite people at this point.

Security had ordered a work crew for tomorrow, but that didn't stop the rest of the regular office staff from feeling shaken, and leaving early. Not Cora, of course. She hung out until she was good and ready to leave, which was well after everyone else. Hell, the only reason Coach went home for the evening at all was because he knew I'd stay to make sure she got home okay, even if I hadn't cleared the bit of information with her first.

Cora kept creeping toward me, one small step at a time. I held myself still, barely daring to breathe as she encroached on my space and finally stopped her advance a half foot in front of me. If she took a deep inhale, her luscious breasts that her crop barely contained would brush my singlet beneath my own Chimera hoodie.

"What the hell makes you think I'd welcome you following me home, Chimera?' she asked, her voice low and breathy.

I stared down at her. "Better me than a rogue camera man ready for tomorrow's four a.m. edition," I stated plainly. That comment seemed to snap her out of it, but I wasn't ready to let her go that easily. I held out my hand palm up. "Phone."

"What?"

"Give me your phone, butterfly."

"No." She backed up a step.

I raised my hand and slid my fingers through her silky blonde hair to massage her nape. "Your phone." I held my other palm out at her waist height, waiting for her to shriek and yank away from me.

She didn't.

Something cold and heavy dropped into my

hand. I nodded without taking my eyes off hers, still massaging her neck. She tossed her head restlessly, and batted once at my arm, but she didn't push my touch away.

Good.

"Code, butterfly."

"Why do you call me that?"

I waited as she blew out a breath.

"Four-seven-four-six-two-four," she muttered. Her cheeks blazed as I entered the numbers as she spoke.

I frowned. "I'm guessing that's not your birthday, butterfly." I knew it wasn't.

"Itspellsgrinch," she muttered, dipping her chin as her words ran together.

I stopped my massage, rearranging my hand to catch her jaw in my fingers and tip her head up to meet my gaze. "Say that again for me, Cora?" I heard her, but from the way color stained her cheeks, I had to get her to repeat it. What could I say? Sadism was one of my kinks.

"It spells *grinch*," she confessed, her voice ringing clear as fucking day across the empty parking lot. "I hate Christmas, okay? Are you happy now?" She wrenched her chin out of my hand. "Can I go now?" Her eyebrows raised as she offered me a look of pure derision mixed with defiance.

Good that you know who holds the reins here.

I nodded thoughtfully. "Have your run, Cora. I'll watch you."

Her skittish look left me in a fresh dose of arousal as she bounced once on her toes and took off without stretching. That was partially my fault, but she'd wear the punishment for it at a later date anyway.

I saved the number I had airdropped from her phone to mine and sent her a text message.

> HEATH: Your ass looks good when you run.

I walked to my bike, the seat still slightly warm from her touch, and started the engine. The sound shattered the silence as I pocketed my phone only to feel it vibrate as she responded to my poke about her form.

> CORA: That's sexual assault, Chimera. A policy you should be intimately familiar with by now.

I barked a hollow laugh. Hell, the whole night had been a sexual assault case in the making, and this was the first time she trotted that card out? Gutsy, but I was prepared for it. If my job was lost to that, then sure, I'd wear it. Not happily, but sure.

HEATH: I'll make sure you get home safe no matter what, butterfly. You can fire me in the morning, if you like.

CORA: And if I told you to go to hell right now and not come anywhere near my home?

HEATH: Is that what you're saying, butterfly?

CORA: ...

CORA: ...

CORA: Thank you for the coffee. It was my favorite. The bagel too.

HEATH: You're welcome.

I pocketed my phone and pulled away from the office, heading to where she lived in a downtown apartment, alone. Half a block back from hers I reversed into an alley, keeping to the shadowed side. Making sure it was unoccupied, I turned off my bike a few moments before she rounded the block's corner.

Hell, Cora must have sprinted that last few hundred meters to make it home that fast. Either I'd rattled her that much, or...

I'd rattled her in another way altogether.

I tossed my phone in my hand as she stopped out the front of her building, and turned in a circle, checking the streetscape. Her gaze lingered on the shadows where I stood, but she didn't seem to see me, lingering for only a second before moving along.

I opened her messages and sent another.

HEATH: Run, Cora. I'm watching.

CORA: Why do you want to see me run?

HEATH: It's my favorite game.

HEATH: One day I might even chase you.

Cora looked up from her phone, staring straight at me, I swore.

I pressed call as she backed up into the apartment building with its lit stairwell that wound up and up, all the way to the top floor. She picked up, her breathing ragged, but didn't say anything. She knew it was me. For a minute, neither of us spoke.

Then I laughed, and she ran.

Winding her way up the stairwell, clutching her phone like a lifeline in full visual range of me as I laughed softly as she ran and ran and ran.

I watched until she exited the stairwell, the breaths coming fast, so ragged. Her keys trembled, rattling metal on metal as she fumbled the lock and swore. Her door opened and slammed. Her shattering breaths broke on a sob as she crashed against something heavy.

I imagined her pressed to the door or the wall inside her apartment, clutching her phone and her keys, an utter, sweating, dripping, panting mess.

My cock hardened as I gripped myself tight, willing myself not to cum as I held my ground. "Are you alright, Cora?" I asked softly.

She let out another sob, though her breaths were gentler now, less ragged. Breathier. "Yes, Valentine. I'm okay."

"You're inside? All locked up?"

"I—No. Wait for me?"

"I'm here."

The lock rattled again. A chain, maybe. I counted the locks with her, humming softly when she swore.

"The locks are done."

"Good girl," I cooed. "I'm so fucking proud of you. That was hard. A really fucking long run, and you're inside, all safe. Have some water. Do you want me to stay until you crawl into bed?"

She hesitated and I wondered for a moment if I'd lost her.

"Y–yes please," she confessed in the barest whisper.

"It's alright. I'm here," I promised her. "Do you want to get water in the dark or do you need lights on?"

"Dark," she whispered again, like she wanted to keep this secret between us, and the lights would blare it to smithereens.

"It's okay, then. Keep a hand on the wall, Cora. Find the kitchen. Two hands for the glass. Put me on speaker," I instructed her.

"Got it," she mumbled a moment later, the sound of water filling a glass obscuring her voice.

"Good. Drink as much as you need. Shower?" I doubt she could think beyond her bed right now.

"In the morning. I'm exhausted."

"It's been a huge day," I murmured. "Where do you keep your nightdress?" I had no idea what attire she slept in.

"Nothing." Material rasped on her skin, her breaths short again. "I don't wear anything to bed."

"Butterfly," I growled a warning. "Get the fuck into bed, curl up and tell me you're safe for the night before I start knocking on doors to find yours."

I knew which one was hers, but she didn't need to know that tonight.

"Sixteen B." More material rasped against skin. *The sheet.* "Goodnight, Valentine."

"Christ, Cora. We're gonna have a talk about your safety habits." I swore liberally, the speaker on mute for a few moments, and scared a stray cat.

"Tomorrow." She yawned in my ear. "You can jog with me."

I laughed softly. "Goodnight, Miss Cora."

"Goodnight, Valentine. Hate me tomorrow."

"I can do that," I promised without venom.

I'd find plenty to hate about her tomorrow. But for tonight, she was the most incredible fantasy I'd ever fucking found.

Utter perfection.

For tonight, Cora Brooks was mine.

I waited in the shadows outside her building, listening to her fall asleep through the speaker until the battery died on her end, then headed home to rub my cock raw to the images of all the things I'd punish her for soon.

So fucking soon.

After we hated each other for a little longer. After she ran from me some more.

After I chased her a while longer.

But damn if we wouldn't have a whole lot of fun together.

CHAPTER FOUR

CORA

I stood outside Corinne Weather's house, and knocked on her door for the ninth time. I had a limit; I just hadn't reached it yet. Because she was home, and I flat out refused to give up. My assistant, Liz, who rarely saw work because the control freak in me required—well, control, stood behind me, tapping out notes on her tablet.

"Do you want me to try around the back?"

I shook my head. "Miss Weathers?" I tipped my head to one side when a shadow passed across the frosted glass pane. "Please open the door. I'm not the press."

The shadow paused. *Okay. So she's as over the media storm as we are.* Not that I blamed her, but if she'd just speak to me, maybe we could help each other.

I inhaled, counted to ten of Liz's taps, and tried again. "I'm a friend of Val— Heath's," I caught the slip at the last minute.

"You know Heath?" The door opened a crack, and a mousy looking woman bearing a patchwork of semi-faded discolored bruises and scratches. The bite marks were still visible.

I attempted a smile that didn't match any other part of me right then and stepped sideways in a shitty attempt to shield Liz—fuck knew, why, she'd seen the tabloids when Corinne's injuries were fresh.

"Yes. I hoped you might help me help him. Please?"

Corinne Weathers frowned. "Is he in trouble? For–for helping me?" The door started to close.

"No–yes," I adjusted my line of thought to see if it would get me where I needed to be. She seemed protective of him. I knew Stockholm syndrome wasn't real but...maybe in this case..? "I don't want him to lose his job—" *True.* "—but right now, it's in real jeopardy if he doesn't start sharing what happened that night."

Also true. I just didn't share the fact that the person he and the team were in jeopardy was from was *me.*

"He didn't hurt me." The rise in her tone and volume left me wishing I could take a step back, and I was pretty sure Liz actually did, though she rallied rather fast from the flurry of footsteps that backed me up again. "Heath was— he—"

I leaned forward, intent on getting this one more self out of her. Nine sets of raps on the weatherboard, peeling house, a whole lot of calling, and worrying the media would set up a fresh picket line the entire time set a fresh fire under my butt.

"I'd love to know more, Corinne," I said softly, attempting to remain impartial despite my growing desperation to find out what the hell had actually happened that night and somehow, impossibly, *make it right.* "But unless someone speaks to me about that night—" A pen poked my ribs. I twitched and sent an irritable look over my shoulder, turning my attention back to the door. "Like I said, I need to know—" The poke came again, this time twice as hard. I bit my lip but when a hand gripped my shoulder, pulling me backward, I snapped. "What the hell?"

A shadow stalked into the space where I stood a moment before. Liz pressed to my back.

"That's Valentine, right?" she breathed in my ear.

I could only nod as Heath sent me an indecipherable look. Our gazes clashed for a long moment that halted time, and in his coal eyes I read both concern and disappointment. Then he turned away, and pressed a hand to the door.

Corrine let Heath Valentine into her house without a word. The door shut after him, the locks snicking with a sense of finality as we were left outside.

I wasn't sure what hurt more—the fact that the man who was accused of hurting her just walked into her house with no resistance whatsoever, or the fact that his disappointment in me mattered more than a door shut in my face in the middle of an investigation.

I stared at the peeling pale blue door for a few seconds longer like it might open once more and admit the Chimera who had disappeared into the depths of the house.

Spoilers: he didn't.

"Let's go," I said brusquely, fighting the tears that prickled the corners of my eyes.

Fuck it, I would *not* cry over some puck boy who barely knew my name.

Liar, liar, lox bagel on fire.

The fact that he had gone out of his way to find out what I liked and watched me last night rankled. On top of today, of all things.

Plus, he was going to lose his job, his place on the team, if I didn't get the answers I sought. I'd be the one to do that to him, alongside Coach. *Me.* And that would hurt because...

I cared.

Damnit, I cared about Heath Valentine. Probably for a similar stupid reason that Corinne Weathers let him into her house.

I released a groan as I reached my car, settling into the driver's seat and rested my forehead on my steering wheel.

"Do you want me to drive?" Liz offered.

"No, but thank you for the offer. I need to do something stupid."

"Like get a Chimera off your mind?" She waggled her eyebrows suggestively at me when I raised my head and started the car.

I pretended not to hear her. Pretended not to think about Valentine following me home last night. Him talking to me as I trembled my way through my dark apartment, locking up, getting water.

He's a predator.

But a caring one.

Gah, it was all so fucked up inside my head. Because if he had asked me to let him in last night, I absolutely would have let him.

But that was last night, and this was now. "No." I straightened and flicked my pony tail over my shoulder. "Like get back to work, ignore Valentine's life choices and work this through."

Screw him, and screw his choices. I had my own to make. That just wouldn't involve him if he didn't involve me. Petty, but then, hadn't we said last night that we would go back to hating each other today?

Wish granted.

"That doesn't seem so stupid to me," Liz muttered, checking her mail on her tablet as I pulled away from the curb, hot spotting off my phone.

My lips formed into a grin that could have been a grimace instead. "Not yet. But I'll make sure we get there before the day's end."

And I'd make sure Valentine knew it, too. I was cruel like that when I didn't get my way. Or bratty. Yep. Totally bratty. If Valentine wanted to play games with me, then I'd play. Bonus round: I'd get my job done as well. Win/win, and all in my favor.

Just the way I liked it.

* * *

"Did you think you could walk into a traumatized woman's house and get away with asking her what the hell happened?"

Both my eyebrows winced on my behalf as I Coach berated my lack of discretion earlier in the day.

"Call it desperation," I muttered, staring at the desk and knowing full well that they should be on this side of it. "You know what the next steps are."

I mean, it would help if I knew what the hell had happened in the first place as I was still fizzy on the details, as, it seemed, was everyone else in the hockey world. All I knew was that I walked back into Ward's office—my office, for the week— and found yet another news interview with Hux talking intently to an anchorman about the incident that he hadn't even freaking attended.

And all without authorization from the club.

Apparently, the players decided to go rogue on this one. Heads would roll.

"Who?"

"You know who."

"Fuck." Coach rubbed a hand over his face,

never breaking eye contact with me once I raised my head and stared him down. "Fuck. You've got the balls to match this team, you know that."

"It's why I'm here, after all."

"It's not the only reason," he argued. "You're supposed to figure out how to get into their heads, work through the points and set them up with a better public face. Sort this shit out." He waved at the oversized screen he'd dragged into his spartan office to display the interview that, no matter the intent, would condemn at least one player.

Valentine.

And no cupid's arrow or pretty row of hearts would save that sexy player's tight ass this time around. We both knew that.

"That's all you want me to do, huh?" I held Coach's gaze unflinchingly, not looking at the distraction of Hux that he offered in his own bid for desperation. "Even when the team bands together and pull stunts like this?"

Coach blew air through his teeth. "*Especially* when they do this shit, Cora. This is them hurting. Needing a protector. I can only do that on the ice. Right now, they need a hero. Do you need a goddam cape? Because today, their hero has to be *you*."

I smirked despite the overwhelming sense of responsibility that slammed into my gut. The mask I had to wear before it all grew too much.

I can't save him and he's relying on me.

No, I had to find a way. That's the message that Coach sent to me.

"Alright," I said softly. "Then I need someone to tell me what the fuck happened, so that I can fix the mess they started." I gathered my files scattered across the desk, the pictures and black and white print blurring for the amount of times I'd read over them. "If they don't trust me, how can I help them?"

"Cora, look at me." Ward matched my tone. "Sweetheart," —I knew it wasn't derogatory, that pet name, and I stopped, giving him the attention he deserved for the hours he put in with the team he loved as much as I did— "Heroes don't just save people who trust them. Those arrogant fuckers out there? When I first came on board, they hated me. Every last one. Right through to the playoffs. Do you know how many games that is in a season? No, don't count. It's a fucking lot, is what it is. Not one or two or three or four. Or even twelve. It's daily practices with them bitching me out. Kicking players off the team who don't make the cut. Subbing them through

Injuries. Scandals just like this one. Hell, you were with me for the last of those. We weathered that one together."

I frowned. "Yeah, you stood between me and them like a brick wall and wouldn't fucking move." I remembered that all too well. "You wouldn't let me talk to them alone. I felt like a teacher about to do something wrong with your ...squad."

I'd felt dirty afterwards and questioned all my life choices. Months later I'd looked back on that time and wondered if that hadn't been Ward's point. Then, I accepted it and moved forward. Now, I wondered again if I hadn't screwed up.

"They hated on me so bad through that." Coach grinned widely. "Solace slashed my tires twice. Hux threatened to quit the team altogether. You know what I did?"

"What?" I knew he didn't report that to the club or the police, because I'd never heard about the incidents until now, which meant no one had. He'd kept those secrets locked to his chest. I wondered what else no one knew about the team and where this speech was headed.

"I promoted Hux to captain. Gave him the responsibility he needed to take the team to the win."

"You took the team to the championships," I

objected. "I used to sit and watch those practices every morning at four a.m. as inspiration. Because if you could all get up and train that hard, then I should be working on PR strategy for you all."

Coach nodded. "We know, and we saw you."

That stopped me. "What?"

"They know, Cora. They respect you, even if right now they don't trust you. Want that cape?"

I stared a moment longer, then kept gathering my things. "I'll buy my own. A fucking sparkly one," I muttered.

Ward laughed softly. "Good girl," he murmured.

Goosebumps rippled along my arms as I grabbed my files and beelined for the door, ignoring Coach's amused look when I ducked past him and almost ran into a wall of Chimera just outside. The scent of pure ambrosia hit me at chest level.

I grabbed the coffee in its reusable bamboo take-away cup without thinking and looked up into Valentine's smokey black eyes.

"That was some speech," he murmured, staring down at me without blinking.

"He's had some practice on you assholes," I managed, clinging to my files and my coffee without wearing or dropping either.

"That last line is mine, Cora. Not his. Remember that."

I nodded, backing up and made it down the hallway without dropping a single thing or ruining my panties, but damn, it was a close thing.

These Chimeras were murder.

Or maybe just one.

CHAPTER FIVE

HEATH

"I've got bad news and good news," Coach announced at the end of practice the same afternoon as I watched Cora wiggle her perfectly curved ass down the club's office hallway and disappear into the kitchen for refuge.

I didn't follow her in there, though it was a close thing, the need to hunt her down and finish what started earlier in the week. Hell, a whole lot longer ago than that, though she didn't need to know just how long my obsession with curves had been going on. Not...yet.

Coach didn't wait for the team's response as we finished up our last drill, but he did motion me over, handing me his phone without looking. I took it the same way, not watching the video that scrolled along in my periphery with the sound turned down. We'd get to that in a moment.

"The bad news is that Solace is out of the rest of the season. We'll see how that injury tracks next year."

Shit. That doesn't sound good.

Coach led up his hands against the muted groans that were bitten off as Hux straightened and banged his stick against the ice. Just once, and silence reigned for the man who knew his best friend wasn't returning to the team this season, or maybe not at all.

"The good news is that we have a goalie who works his ass off for you on the ice and off it. Valentine's not going anywhere, no matter what the media says." He nodded, and that was it. End of talk. He skated sideways. "Watch the video."

Coach moved away, grabbing Shannon and Hux and snapping out strategy in his typical rapid fire succession manner as he usually did. Both players quietened to listen as I dipped my attention to the phone in my hand and restated the video.

Cora's sassy face and powerhouse body language filled the screen as she presented to a media crew outside the building. Not so long ago, looking at the light and shadows behind her. But the backdrop wasn't what caught my attention. It was her energy that seemed to seep through the screen at me, and suddenly I understood why Coach handed me his phone.

Gliding across the ice toward the bench, away from the rest of the team, I inched the sound up just enough to make out her words without being over-heard by everyone else. Something told me to keep the moment private, at least for now.

Cora's eyes hardened as she talked, her energy literally glowing around her, or maybe that was the sun setting in her face, or the media's constant flashes going off as she spoke. Nothing seemed to deter her as I tuned in halfway through her talk.

"...the Chimeras have worked to maintain their reputation of clean, hard and passionate players. All year, the team has trained hard. I know that, because I've been there with them. Watched when they turned up each morning—every single player, including the neophyte, who has certainly earned his nickname." She paused for effect and the well trained media crew tittered on cue.

Fuck, she had them, and me, eating out of her hand. Damn, just the image of kneeling for her and licking her fingers—and other body parts—left me hard enough in my kit that I groaned. Biting my lip to hear her, I palmed myself but my cup got in the road and I ached all the same. Christ, it was like being trapped in a chastity device, a torture designed by her. I inhaled deeply and tried to focus on her words.

Cora waited for the media—and apparently, me —to settle before she spoke again. "This week's media mess has been just that, a sensationalism brought about by the people in front of me." She leaned forward with her hand cupped around her mouth as though imparting a secret. "That's you lot, if you have no idea what I'm saying and you can record me, lynch me, or fuck right off. I don't care." She straightened, and her smile was nothing shy of viscous. "This is my team. These are my colors. Chimeras are made of many differing parts to create a larger, magnificent beast. Today you get to see a different side than usual. But from now on when you report about *my* team, you report the correct news on what *my* players do. Thank you. No questions."

Cora waited one second longer in the hell of flashes and instantaneous chatter that erupted despite her declaration that must have been beyond shitty to experience, and turned, walking sedately off screen.

My stomach swooped as I took in her attire, her

casual walk, her sneakers with her knee length skirt that showed her curved legs, hips and her team colors displayed beneath her suit jacket.

As she walked, she rolled her shoulders back and let that jacket fall to the ground, never stopping to pick it up. And all the media saw was her back, and the reverse side of the Chimeras jersey she wore.

The jersey bearing the number eighty-three. I didn't have to look at the name above it before my skates were moving without my permission. I jammed the phone back into Coach's hand, remembering the pretty speech he gave her and wondered if he realized what the hell sort of outcome he'd forced when he told her that not all heroes wore capes.

No, they just donned their team's colors.

Because in making that little speech of her own, talking like she did to the media, Cora Brooks took the Chimeras out of the firing line. She did everything she was paid to do—but in return, she became the sacrifice. And she knew full well what she was doing when she talked out *her* team and *her* colors, making a stand in their faces, defying what they had done to us.

Now instead of my job on the line, it was her job and her reputation instead.

"Fucking hell," I groused, kicking the door the to the player's bench open.

I grabbed my kit, already pulling my protective layers off before I hit the changing room. I needed to have a word with my girl. Because she was my girl, no matter the fact that we'd never publicly claimed each other yet, other than me buying her a few coffees and feeding her up because she flat out refused to look after herself and worked too damn hard for a team who refused to love her for the sacrifice she just made on our behalf.

Well, maybe she had claimed me, seeing as that was my number emblazoned on her back that the media captured that would be spread all over tonight's tabloids, and my name across her shoulders.

Damnit, I needed to get her coffee before she ran herself dry. Needed to warn her of what the hell she'd just done if she didn't already realize. But first, there was someone else I needed to speak to, and she needed to understand what Cora just did on her behalf, too.

I waited outside Cora's borrowed office, holding her coffee and snack, her jacket draped over my arm.

She'd left it in the parking lot and never gone back to get it at all. Another form of silent protest, perhaps. I admired that about her, though I wasn't sure if she had a pure stubborn streak or a run of defiance that rippled through her soul. Either way was sexy as hell, but only one spelled *B-R-A-T*.

But the office was empty when I returned from my quick pot practice chance and handful of errands bearing gifts for my Chimeras goddess, and so I waited, praying that her coffee wouldn't get too cold in my hands and that I'd be up for another run before she returned.

My phone buzzed in my pocket. I knew it would be Coach, but he also knew I had business to straighten out before I could deal with anything else for today. Because for today, everything else would just have to wait. He could bust my balls on the ice with as many pucks as he and the rest of the team could throw at me tomorrow.

This afternoon and the rest of my evening would be for worship at the feet of the woman I had craved for far too long.

Cora barreled at her typical speed along the corridor, talking into her phone cramped against her ear as she clutched two text books—-fuck knew what for—to her chest, along with a stack of manilla folders. Coach loved those fuckers. No wonder they got along so well.

I grabbed her phone, placed her coffee in her hand and nudged the office door open with my foot.

She stared up at me with wide eyes, but never stopped talking. "Yes, I can do this evening. No, I won't be drinking. Why? Because it's midweek, and I have practi— yes, I was fuck— ah. Yes. I was serious on the talk. Yes, I do practice with them. No, you li— No, I am not a Chimera. Yes, I work seated in the stands. I don't think that's appropriate, do you?" She sighed and sank into the chair I pulled out of her, letting me rest my hands onto her shoulders as she finally off loaded everything onto the desk.

My fingers sank into taut muscles. A soft groan left her as she leaned back into my touch, then stiffened. I massaged her shoulders gently, then a little deeper. Minute by minute she relaxed.

"Alright, fine. Tonight." Another sigh. "Yes, I'll— where? Jesus Christ. I'm not seventeen with a fake ID, Pe–. Yes, alright. I'll go if that's the spot. Fine." She hung up, dropped her phone to the desk and followed up with her forehead. "Fuck. Me."

"I'd love to."

"Stop it, Valentine," she grumped at me, as I rearranged her arms beneath her head, creating a pillow and worked on her neck. The next sound to come from her was a low moan.

I glanced at the office door that swung shut from the outside with a gentle click, but I doubted she noticed, lost in whatever the hell that conversation was. "I saw your speech."

"You saw...Oh, shit." The girl who relaxed in my hands stiffened.

I traced along the collar of her semitransparent blouse that most definitely wasn't my jersey. "Did you take my number from my locker?"

She shook her head. "No?"

"Liar," I breathed, leaning lower to inhale along her nape. *Fuck,* I could smell the muskiness along her, knew she hadn't showered afterward. *Best turn on in the damn world.* "Do you still have it?"

"Y-yes," she confessed, gripping the edge of the desk with both hands until her knuckles turned white.

"Keep it. I have a spare." *One.* But fuck it. For her I'd shell out for a whole wardrobe to be made up. "I told you we needed a talk about you and security. That little chat...It just made you a target, Cora."

She sighed and settled on the desk. "That was the idea."

I stopped rubbing her shoulders. "Keep talking."

"Keep massaging? Right there?"

I laughed. "Talk, Cora."

"Your job was the one that would go," she said bluntly. "I couldn't find a way around that. Not without either you or Corinne talking to me. So, I fixed it."

I swallowed hard. "I would have taken the loss."

"Yeah? And who would be goalie if both you and Solace were out, huh? You think of that, hero?" she spat, pushing her body against me.

I held a hand to her nape and pressed her back to the desk until she whimpered.

"Cora, seeing you up there, alone, wearing my fucking number..." I breathed hard, leaning down to graze my lips along the back of her neck. "Fuck, I almost came in my pants in the middle of training," I murmured. "It was hot as fuck seeing you take them all on alone."

"Oh," she whispered, as I licked the shell of her ear, squirming deliciously beneath me. "Heath, *please—*"

I released her neck, sliding my hand around her throat and pulled her back gently, pinning her to the tall chair back. The leather was the only thing between us as I held her there. She swallowed hard against my hand, still gripping the desk.

"Do you want me to apologize?" she burst into the silence as I held her there, hypnotized by the way her pulse fluttered frantically against the pads of my fingers.

I smiled, though she couldn't see it and leaned down to press my lips to her temple. "I want you to invite me to your party tonight. So you're not alone again. I want you to ask me to come with you, so that I can watch you while you're out, watch you walk home. Watch you when you walk up the stairs of your apartment building. Know when you leave your door unlocked for me to come in tonight. Will you do that for me, Cora? Or do you want to not ask me to go, and I'll watch you anyway?"

Her pulse ratcheted up a notch, her thighs spreading as she twisted in my hold. Breaths came faster as she arched and I swore she'd come if I held on to her any longer. *Fuck it.* Risking everything she'd just put in place just to test a theory, I tightened my hold on her throat a fraction. Not enough to steal her air, just enough to remind her who we were together.

Cora's head tipped back, giving me access to her entire body as her legs fell open on the chair. The scent of her permeated the room, sweet and liquid heat. I ached to draw my fingers through her swirling heat but I wanted to see if she'd lose herself without being touched. Just from the mere idea of what we could be together.

It didn't take long.

Her back arched, tits thrust out against that semi-transparent top. Her nipples were hard beneath her bra, the pebbled tips straining as she moaned for me. Her lips opened, inviting and sweet. I leaned down and dribbled a line of drool gently into her mouth. She swallowed, her eyes dozy as she tasted me and—

Cora sighed, coming apart beneath my hold as my saliva slid down her throat and her slick coated Coach's worn chair. Her thighs trembled, out of control, hips bucking gently. The softest sounds slid from her lips, and my cock strained in response. I willed my orgasm back as she lost herself in her own, sighing her release, boneless in my hand.

I stroked her pulse point, gentling my hold to caress her. "So fucking beautiful and good for me, Cora," I praised her. I leaned down and licked my saliva from her lips. "Now ask nicely and I'll be there tonight for you."

"Come and be my Chimera protector tonight," she whispered, her hands dropping between her things with another sweet sigh.

I smiled, cupping her breast and squeezed

gently. "I'll be there, whether you see me or not, Cora. Come for me twice on this chair. Two fingers, knuckles all the way. Deal?"

"Deal," she sighed, burrowing her fingers into her juicy as fuck cunt and sloshing for me.

"Fuck you're so good." I wanted to watch her but I needed to sort my own shit for tonight. "Send me where I need to be for you, understand?"

"Yes, Valentine," she whispered, nodding as I set up her phone with video, streaming it live to myself so I could watch her finger herself until she came.

Christ, she was stunning. And now, she was mine.

CHAPTER SIX

CORA

I smiled inanely at the media crew, pretending to laugh at yet another not-funny joke the journalist in front of me made and didn't pretend to look for Valentine.

Not here. Still.

Or again. But Coach was, leaning his gray headed frame against the bar, looking completely out of place in jeans, a dark blue shirt and scowl that matched no one else in the club.

I couldn't work out what was worse: the fact that Coach was left on babysitting duty for the night, or that after all the intimacy and show ponying that we shared earlier in the afternoon, Valentine stood me up.

That's what you get for falling for your not-fling of two days, Cora.

The little voice in the back of my head promised me that I was insane for getting involved in the work-place romance—*sexmance?*—that I swore I never would in the first place. And of all Chimeras, I'd chosen Valentine. Or rather, he had chosen me.

I wasn't sure if I should be insulted by that last or not, but here we were and... It appeared that I had chosen him right back.

More than chosen for the way that I ignored the media crew I had, somewhat stupidly, agreed to drinks with after my little performance outside the Chimera's office this afternoon. Stupid, because Valentine had been in my space at the time and my brain refused to function correctly around him.

But also because I was supposed to be picking the brain of this group for *why* they had targeted the Chimeras when they had left the team alone for so long. Pure boredom? Collusion on a slow print week? I didn't understand it when the woman made no statement and all we had was Valentine escorting a woman, albeit battered, from the club. This club, as it happened.

I placed my drink back on the table and rose.

"Not thirsty?" Peatie, my usually-tame media spy, appeared at my side on cue. "Atmosphere's a bit low for now. Should be pumping later!"

So was he—jacked up on something. The dilated pupils gave it away if his loud voice and hyper attitude didn't.

I shrugged, needing to get away from him and this afternoon's bad choices as soon as I could. "Not right now, Peatie," I muttered, pushing forward, between him and another journalist who watched me thoughtfully. A hand landed on my arm as I made my escape, halting me mid step.

I froze and looked back, pasting a fake smile across my face. "I'm just headed for the loo."

"Sure. But you're the girl who gave the speech this afternoon. That took some balls. Kudos to you." He watched me carefully.

I watched him, back and very slowly extracted my arm. "Thanks."

Peatie speed talked all the way to the bar where I left him, still chattering to Coach who looked like he was ready to rip[me a new one. Even I wasn't sure if Peatie knew the difference between Coach and me at this point.

"Where's Valentine?" I mouthed to Coach,

glancing over my shoulder as I scanned the club that was still sparsely enough populated that a giant hockey player couldn't hide in the population.

I lied. Valentine would never hide in this crowd, or any other.

"No fucking idea," Coach yelled in a moment of silence right between songs.

I closed my eyes and died a little death right on the spot. With my eyes still closed I turned around, hand headed for the toilets. One step and I ran smack into a warm, hard body, bumping my nose on what felt like a brick wall.

"Fu–ow," I muttered. "Sorry." I opened my eyes and sidestepped the blackout that refused to let me around.

"Cora. Where are you going?" An amused voice held me prisoner.

No wait, that was his hands grazing my hips.

"Uh. I was going to powder my....something?" I peeked up at Valentine through my lashes, willing myself not to cower before him.

At work, I wore work makeup. I wore a work suit and, apart from my stint donning his jersey, I wore only Chimera appropriate clothing.

Right now, nothing about me was appropriate

whatsoever. And I made that choice knowingly and willing when I stepped outside my door.

Suddenly, the oversized blonde curls, the cropped blue leather jacket zipped to my bust and my ice blue beaded mini dress with the deep v to my navel seemed like a really, really stupid idea.

Or maybe, from the way he surveyed my body in the slowest once over in history, possibly the most dangerous one.

"Do you really need to powder anything, Cora, or were you escaping?" Valentine asked in a low tone, though he blocked my path to the toilets.

"Escaping?" I squeaked my confession like a spring church mouse. "Still escaping," I added hopefully in a more regular voice.

"No chance, Butterfly."

His hand folded around my blue leather covered elbow, towing me back to the bar. Ward stood alone, no Peatie in sight, blessedly.

"Where'd your sidekick go?" I asked as Valentine released my arm and my voice returned to its usual volume.

Coach's gaze slid between us, narrowing. "You 'friend' wandered off, talking to a chair."

I frowned. "I don't see a chair."

Coach shrugged. "Neither could he."

"That kinda night already, huh?" Valentine squeezed my arm again, and placed a bottle of water in front of me.

I tested the lid, smiling when I found it still screwed tight and uncracked. "Thank you." I beamed at him.

"Wherever it takes. Who was your friend?" he asked curiously. "You have...interesting taste?"

I shrugged. "My media spy. Usually he feeds me interesting information but today he's been a feature article in himself." Peatie's hangover in the morning would be of epic proportions. I didn't envy the tomorrow version of himself, and I doubted he would either, if he had two brain cells that would rub together right now.

The club slowly filled, the Chimeras' coach and Valentine blessedly creating a barrier around me.

"I think I'm supposed to be socializing," I yawned, waving for a bartender.

Valentine's frown was audible from where he stood a few feet back in an obvious attempt not to touch me in front of his coach. "I thought you weren't drinking tonight."

There was no judgement in his tone, simply a

question, about my own judgement or my motives perhaps.

I sent him a bratty grin, wondering what he was like if I pushed him. Hey, a girl needed hobbies. Leaning forward, I cupped my hands to disguise my order and yelled into the bartender's ear. I doubted Valentine heard me; the club's volume took it up a notch the moment it turned eleven o'clock and well past all our bedtimes with a predawn start in a few hours.

Apparently Peatie wouldn't be the only one regretting tomorrow.

"What's that about?" Valentine's fingers traced the blue leather at my wrist.

Coach shook his head, muttering. "I'm going to bed. Don't stay out late. Or go home together, for fuck's sake. Next week, maybe," he growled, glaring at us.

I laughed as my drink order arrived in a double shot glass.

Coach sent me a second exasperated look. Another was directed over my head I didn't bother to interpret, and walked away.

"Cora," Valentine murmured in warning as I tested my shot glass and sighed.

I crooked a finger that I dipped into the dark, cold liquid. "Come here." I wiggle the finger in the air, speaking to him loudly over the music as someone jostled me.

Warm hands slid beneath my jacket to hold me steady as Valentine regarded me with a steady gaze. "I don't drink."

"Trust me?"

His head cocked to one side, he opened his mouth. I smiled as I traced his bottom lip with my fingertip, then on impulse touched the tip of his tongue.

Warmth enveloped my finger as he sucked gently on the tip and suddenly my wardrobe choices were very obvious and really fucking bad.

Really bad.

"Jesus," I whispered, not pulling my finger back as he cleaned the tip and released me.

I dropped my hand between us, watching his eyes. His pupils were blown wide with arousal and I knew mine would be the same.

"Cora," he murmured my name.

Not that I heard him, but I read my name on his lips.

Lips I wanted on mine. On my body. Licking me.

I'm so gone for this man.

I gripped the zip on my jacket, suddenly glad Coach had left for the night, and pulled it down, wiggling my arms free. Valentine never moved his hands from my waist as I stripped my outer layer off, handing it to the bartender, leaving me in the dress I'd chosen, thinking it was cute and sexy.

The way he drank in the beaded, strapless dress with its plummeting v to my navel held up with some tape and my boobs, told me it was a mistake and that he was seconds away from mauling me at the bar.

I wiggled my butt. "I'm going to dance," I said without yelling. My voice strained as I moved my mouth clearly for him to read my lips. "Are you coming with me, or are you going to watch?"

He waited a minute, so long I thought he might not answer me. That I'd scared him, or that he would reject me.

Valentine leaned in, his lips brushing my ear. "Both, Cora. Dance for me."

I shivered as he squeezed my hand and let me lead him away from the bar. People who would have jostled me didn't. I followed in the wake that opened behind him, tucked away in the calm that he created. A shiver passed over me as the amount of pure *trust* that I put into this man slammed me.

Then he spun me into his chest, warmth

pervading my front. I stared up at him, and everything, including the ability to breathe or think, was forgotten.

Valentine's broad, strong hands skated over my hips, his touch so light as to not disturb the swinging beads on my dress. "Move for me," his lips said as I read them through the pulsing beat even though I couldn't hear his words.

My body moved as commanded. For a moment, the visibility of being in front of a crowd with him, the eyes of everyone around us seemingly locked on him and possibly me too for being with a Chimera, left me almost stationary in place. Then, as his eyes darkened with heat, and his heat dipped to crowd me on the fast filling dance floor, my hips began to sway in his hold. I tipped my shoulders back, my eyes drifting shut.

And in the space he made for us, the club with its darkened spaces and caffeine eating into my veins, I danced, as promised.

Just for him.

Valentine never grabbed me or crushed me against him, his hands grazing over my dress with the utmost respect in his touch. My nipples ached and pebbled as tight as the beads on my dress when he stroked the undersides of my breasts that grew heavy when he did nothing more. His breath brushed my lips, and I opened my mouth, willing him to kiss me as my body curled and undulated, moving in a rhythm designed, I swore, just for him.

"Cora," he rasped, close enough, *low enough*, for me to hear.

My eyes cracked open to find him arched over me, hands closed so freaking lightly around my waist. Hands that could crush me, bruise me, if he so chose.

But he didn't.

Heath Valentine was all about control over violence, and his touch, or lack of it, was—

Electric.

The tip of his tongue stroked my bottom lip, wet and hot. I moaned, my mouth open and begging for more of his touch. Hell, I'd come for him in Coach's office with my legs wide open, touched myself and come for him on video that he'd watched live and he hadn't even kissed me properly yet.

The thought left me hotter than ever. Heat gushed between my thighs, slicking me even though he barely touched me now. His tongue stroked my lip in a parody of what else I needed from him, but when I rose up desperately on my toes he just laughed at me and drew back the same amount, making me chase him.

"*Asshole*," I mouthed through a blast of music that was more bass and beat than anything else.

Those dark eyes glittered at me. "Dance, Cora."

I whimpered, pressing against him, grinding helplessly, but it was a one way event. He watched me, as promised, and I knew he liked what he saw because his erection protruded against my belly.

Taking the risk, I rose up onto my toes in my heels again, tilting my head back. "Please," I begged, knowing he could hear me. Probably he couldn't see me, either, as the strobe flashed incessantly, leaving us as nothing more than a series of frozen snapshots in the dark.

His mouth met mine in the barest connection. I closed my eyes, relieved, even though it wasn't the kiss I needed. Not yet but I knew we would get there. I teased the tip of his tongue with mine, but that was all he would give me, tiny touches, light caresses. It was nowhere near enough but that seemed to be his intent, to drive us both mad with need.

Fuck, from the way my thighs slicked, how I pressed my legs together and rubbed against him until he gently held me back with a warning look, it was well and truly fucking well working.

The song ended and I stood before him, panting

and filled with the sort of flush that no amount of recirculated nightclub air could fix.

Apparently, Valentine felt the same way. His hand closed around mine firmly, he drew me through the crowd in longer strides than before. I took two steps to each one of his to keep up as he headed for the door. I looked over my shoulder, seeking the journalist party, then decided I didn't care. It wasn't like I was with them, anyway. Someone called my name, or I thought they did. Valentine's hand tightened on mine, his grip warm and firm.

I raised a hand over my head in what I hoped wasn't too much of a *faux pas* farewell, and breathed in crisp night air that slapped me in the face. The caffeine hit had been nice earlier but the chill air sobered me out of my lust induced haze... for about a second as Valentine led me around a corner that backed onto a half filled parking lot. He wheeled about to face me.

Unslaked need blazed in his face as he closed the short distance between us. What I'd thought before had been all wrong. His hands closed on my waist, squeezing me tightly as he dipped his head and claim my mouth in a fierce kiss that left me breathless and in no doubt that I was well and truly fucked.

Or at least I was about to be, Chimera style.

"Heath," I whispered then faltered, unable to finish my thought as he stared down at me.

"You wanna go back inside with your friends, Cora," he murmured. "Be my guest." His touch dropped away, leaving cold patches on my sides where warmth had bloomed a moment before.

I shook my head, aching to inch forward, but could only lean into his space. My feet were locked into place between shards of broken glass and gravel beneath my heels.

Valentine's breaths were even as he watched me. "You should go home."

"No." I shook my head, adamant. "Why bring me out here if all you wanted was to tell me what to do?"

The corner of his mouth quirked in his rare version of a smile. "I thought you liked it when I told you what to do."

Suddenly I was the one panting as my vision blurred. Damnit I hated being out of control, and I hated that I wanted to run from him like I had in the office corridor. But for some stupid, *really* stupid fucking reason, I needed to stay and duke this one out with him.

Here, tonight.

"You should run." He turned his back to me, one

measured step away, and then another, heading for the black on black bike that I knew was his.

And suddenly I understood what his version of control meant. That it mirrored my panic and that him telling me to *run* didn't mean that at all.

At least, not tonight.

"No." I strode after him, around him and planted a hand firmly on his chest.

The corner of his mouth flickered again. "Reckless, Cora."

He gave me one breath—just one—before his hands closed on my waist again. Then I was airborne as he lifted me onto his bike and laid me back across the seat, looming over me. My breath hitched and I slapped at his chest.

"*No.*"

Valentine froze.

Inch by inch he eased back, though his hands remained on my body. "Be clear, Cora. Right now with me."

I nodded, tossing my hair over my shoulder. The wide curls mussed and fell out but I didn't care as I knelt up on the bike seat. I wobbled, the machine wobbled but his hands were on me and I knew he wouldn't let me fall. That was the level of trust we had.

"You. Here." I pointed to the seat he'd planted me on.

Two eyebrows rose, but he said nothing else as he picked me up and swung me across his lap. I fought that, too, using his momentum to straddle him the moment his denim clad behind hit the leather seat.

"Better." I nodded, letting my thighs slide over his, reveling in the rough sensation of his jeans against my skin, the heat of his body permeating through the material. I leaned forward, resting my hands on his shirt and stared straight into his eyes. This way, we were at the same level. "So much better."

"Fuck, you are a little brat, aren't you?" He squeezed me again, leaning forward to run his nose along mine, inhaling gently.

Then his mouth slammed over mine in a hard kiss, his tongue forcing its way inside. I cried out into his mouth, knowing I flooded his jeans as I rubbed myself against him. Heat overwhelmed me as I got everything I wanted in one. His hands roamed my body roughly.

Beads from my dress pinged off his bike and scattered across the parking lot in tiny shards of shattered frost and reflected ice. I moaned as he pulled my skirt up, baring my thighs.

One hand dipped beneath the curve of my ass, squeezed my thighs hard enough to leave red marks. And other sorts of marks. I moaned at the sensation, undulating to the rhythm he set, his feet planted firmly either side of the bike.

"Fuck, Cora. You're perfect. A handful each side, and—" He broke off, cursing fluently as he reached between my legs and stroked my bare cunt, coming up with fingertips full of wetness. "Christ, butterfly. You're dripping all over my jeans. I hope you'll clean that with your tongue later."

I whimpered against his mouth as he claimed me again, his kisses changing to something more possessive, deeper and slower. I reached between us, palming his cock through his jeans and toyed with the zip he strained against, until he was free in my hand. Thick and long, I wondered for a moment if I hadn't bitten off more than I could take. I closed my hands around his heavy length, the velvet feel of him an absolute luxury.

One glance at his face told me we'd make it work.

"Control it yourself," he murmured as he helped me lift over him, notching himself at my entrance. "Take only how much you want, Cora."

I rubbed the head of his cock against my wetness, getting us both messy. Valentine bit back a groan as I dropped over him, taking as much as I could in a single thrust before I pushed up again. The burn and stretch was *perfect*. My thighs strained but he helped, lifting me to the crown of him, then letting me control the slow glide back down, but only as far as I wanted to go. So full, but I needed more. All of him.

Bracing my weight against his shoulders, I panted after only a few thrusts. "I- I can't–"

"You will," he promised, his eyes as black as night as he lifted me. "Again, Cora. Milk me with that hot, soaking little cunt until I mark you inside as mine."

I moaned, already gushing for him as he rumbled his approval. That noise from his chest left me boneless and I let him lift and guide me, stretching my thighs as I could, tightening my internal muscles on every thrust. His thumbs curled over my clit as he helped me work myself up and it took only a few more moments before I cried out, dropping my head onto his shoulder.

My orgasm shattered me in a moment, the feel of him inside me too much. I slid all the way to the root of him, aided by the fresh slick.

"Good girl, Cora. I'm going to fuck you now," Valentine murmured.

I clung to him as he began to move, lifting us off the bike with his legs spread and then—

I screamed into his shoulder, uncaring if everyone in the street outside the club could hear us. Hell, if any of the journos saw us, we'd be tomorrow's extra headline. I couldn't think up anything right now. Nothing other than Valentine's cock pistoning in and out of me, the friction so much that I bit into his shoulder. He wrapped one hand behind my head, holding me close as he fucked me with the other gripping my ass as he railed me from below.

My screams rippled around the darkened, gritty parking lot as he fucked us both marking me as his, and him as mine.

Valentine slammed deep, his cock thickening as it rippled inside me. His roar against my skin, even muffled, echoed. I shivered in his embrace, willing my pussy to milk him, wanting his seed as deep as I could take him.

Maybe we were both broken. Maybe we were both ruined.

Maybe we were made this way for each other.

He held me close, murmuring soothing things as he licked sweat from the hollows of my throat. "Fuck, you taste delicious, butterfly," he rasped into my skin as he settled back onto the bike.

I mumbled something incoherent, raising bleary eyes to his face.

"And you're fucking beautiful like that. Are you going to run home for me and leave the door unlocked so I can hunt you later?" His deep timbre worked its way bone deep.

I clung to him a moment longer, unwilling to move until he nudged me. "Do I have to let you go?" I murmured sleepily.

His laugh sent fresh ripples through my body, deep enough that we both groaned. "Yes, Cora. Move. before someone sees you and I take them to the hospital. Then you'll have a real problem to fix." The level of possession in his voice left me flushed head to toe. Deep inside me, his cock flexed back to life. "That is, unless you want me to fuck you out here where anyone can see you, rather than love you in your bed later?"

"I'll go," I managed, attempting to swing a leg over his and nearly face planted off his bike into the grit beneath us.

His laughter echoed around us. "Cute, butterfly," he muttered. "Damn, I've fallen for you, you know that?"

"You're not alone." My confession fell in one of

those silent moments right as I managed to swing myself free.

A feral plunging noise filled the absence of sound, and Valentine's cum dripped down my legs.

A fresh wave of humiliation washed over me. Oh, hell. Had I just admitted I was falling for a Chimera? The one I really wasn't supposed to, after everything, and to his face, with his fluids coating me? This was *not. Okay.* I closed my eyes and willed myself to count to ten. Nope. Not working.

Okay, backwards. Yep, that was....shit. I was so totally, utterly fucked. My eyes heated and tears coated my cheeks. Yay, more fluids.

"Cora." Warm hands coated my cheeks, thumbs brushing away my tears when I shook my head and refused to look at him, or anything else. "Cora," he repeated when I didn't answer him.

Can't answer him.

Valentine sighed then his mouth was on mine in a slow, deep kiss that left me in no question where I stood with him.

In deeper than before.

I shuddered in his arms, and leaned closer.

"Better. Now go home." His hands dropped the waist of my ruined dress, squeezing in that same rhythm of his from before. "Go home and run that last part so I can hunt you, butterfly. Leave the door open, and get on the bed, exactly as you are, all freshly fucked and messy. Because tonight I'll love you until the sun comes up, Cora."

"Tomorrow you have early practice." Which I was going to watch with a tired hangover. My promise to myself—if they practiced, I watched. My silent deal with them even if they never agreed to it.

"Tonight is for us. Ours. Do you understand me?" He pressed a kiss to my lips before I could say anything and the only answer I gave was a nod. "Good girl. Now, run home with my cum sliding down my legs and remember every way I just fucked you. How my cock felt inching its way inside your cunt, stretching you out so I'm the only man who'll ever fit you from now on. Rub those beautiful thighs together for me, Cora. Nice and slick. Tonight I'm going to drench you in my cum."

I shuddered, nearly orgasming from his filthy words as he held me tight to him, laughing softly. "Don't leave me alone," I whispered, hating how desperate I sounded. How needy.

"I won't, Cora. Not with me. You'll never be alone."

I sighed, relaxing into his chest at his promise. His chuckle above me and a little push left me cold as his embrace disappeared left me aching and chilled.

"Run, Cora. Remember what I said."

I took one glance at those possessive, glittering black eyes and I did exactly what he said.

I ran.

CHAPTER SEVEN

HEATH

Sparkling aquamarine beads scattered across black gravel in Cora's wake as she stumbled away from me on wobbling legs. Her spiked heels didn't help but I watched her leave, my hand on my cock as I zipped myself up, already hard again with the sight of her frantically trying to comply with my commands.

Run, Cora.

Run home with my cum sliding down your legs.

Fuck, I wanted to open her door, find her on her bed, shove her dress up and slide my hands up her wet thighs. Spread her open and fuck her gently until she shattered and broke beneath me.

Again and again and fucking again until we were both exhausted and covered in each other's juices. The filthier the sex, the better, but with her, what I wanted was simple.

I wanted everything.

I wanted to wake up with her in my arms every morning, see her wearing my jersey when I brought her breakfast and coffee. Kiss her in the office in front of everyone, take her home on the back of my bike.

Most of all I wanted to follow her home as she returned, make sure that she got there safely. But first I needed to collect her jacket that we'd left at the bar. After ruining her dress—I'd buy her a dozen new ones if that's what it took to apologize—I didn't want to throw away any more of her things carelessly.

Only ruining her clothing by design seemed fair, or consensual.

Heading back into the club left me on edge. Despite being the tallest person in it by far, I couldn't stop the images that scrolled through my mind from the last time I'd been in the place, back when I'd found Corinne Weathers in the corner of the men's toilets, sobbing quietly, curled in on herself.

Worst? Three other men walked past her, writing her off as drunk before I stopped and checked if she was okay. One of them was a Chimera. She'd made me promise not to tell who hurt her, fearing the media shitstorm that would follow. I understood, and took that blunt end on her behalf. Hux backed me, and though we refused to talk, I figured Coach got it, too, seeing as he never raked us over the coals for our choices. Sure, he came down hard, but it was par for the course. He could have done or said a whole lot worse, though he never did.

But getting through to Cora was different. She had her heart in the right spot, sure, wanted to defend the girl who was hurt. That part I got. I still questioned her social life choices, but her act today, talking to the journo crew the way she did? That did it for me. I'd already started falling hard for her, my obsession over the top before she started ripping us a new one a few days ago.

Then this afternoon...fuck me. I was hers from the moment she put my number on her back. For as long as she wanted me, and forever after.

I leaned over the edge of the bar and snagged Cora's blue leather jacket, sending a wave to the bartender. He gave me a thumbs up, seeming to recognize my face which still felt weird, but I was starting to understand the life that came with the

Chimera jersey. Hell, if I didn't fuck up this next part, maybe I'd be able to keep it for the rest of the season.

Maybe even a while longer.

Folding Cora's jacket neatly, I tucked the garment under my arm and made my way out of the club without being accosted by anyone, though I scanned the room more than once, searching for a specific face.

Don't fuck it up. Don't fuck it up—

I made a promise to Corinne. I made promises to Coach. The only person I hadn't made that same promise to was Cora, but she was waiting for me. And so, I turned around and left the club, running into a journalist I semi recognized from the press conference Cora hosted earlier in the week.

"Did your girl get home safe?" he demanded, not looking at me. His eyes slid side to side and he pulled out a pack of cigarettes, flicking a lighter nervously though not actually lighting the one that hung from his lips.

"She's none of your business," I said shortly, stepping around the man, intent on getting on my bike and following Cora home.

"She is if she winds up like the other woman. What was her name? Storm? Stormish?"

"Weathers," I said shortly. "You should know. Didn't you write some bullshit story about us?"

He waved my irritation away with a frivolous flick of his nicotine stained fingers. "Part of the job."

I fixed him with a hard stare. The easy rebuttal of *no it's not* stayed locked away behind my lips, thankfully. That his job was made up of pretend stories was akin to mine being made up of creating ice sculptures with a hockey stick. Both were bull-shit, but I wasn't about to get into that with this shady as fuck, inebriated jurno right now.

"What do you want?"

"Did you see her leave?"

I smirked, recalling Cora stumbling away from me, the insides of her thighs glossed with our mixed fluids. "Yeah, I did. What did you need, again?" I pulled my keys out of my pocket and slung one leg over my bike.

He shook his head, apparently trying to focus. *Don't puke on my shoes, paper boy.*

The journo weaved sideways and caught himself on my handlebars. "Yeah, but you're not with her. Did you take her home, or what?"

His fixation on my girl was starting to bother me. "Spit it out, man. I don't have time for—"

"Peatie was asking about her, alright? I tried to

tell him that she was with you, but he left and now I can't find him. Where the hell is she?"

Sounding more sober than he had the entire conversation, the man got up in my face, but suddenly I didn't give a shit about the man's ramblings.

"What name did you say?"

He stepped back at my growl, his hands raised. "Peatie, alright? Her favorite little paparazzi tool who gives her all the insides on us. He's not liked by anyone, none of us on either side. But he's obsessed with her. He has been for fucking years. She doesn't know, and he likes to— Well, he's got this weird kink, you know? He likes to—"

"Bite." The single word snapped between us, brittle as fuck. "Yeah. I fucking know."

My thumb blurred as I threw out a quick message to my girl, my heart in my throat before I started my bike and tore away from the man, showering him with gravel. His curses followed me away from the club, but fucking sue me.

He was right, after all. I needed to make sure Cora got home safe. Suddenly all the banter we had earlier about hunting and leaving the door unlocked for me seemed like the worst fucking idea in history.

Because I knew Peatie's name, just like I knew his particular kink. I'd seen it before.

On Corinne Weathers.

The buildings blurred either side of me as I focused on the road and prayed I made it to her before she did as she promised and left that door wide open with only my message as warning to decipher.

Valentine: RUN, Cora.

I could only hope she'd read it and understand, and lock that damn door. That or I did, before he got there first.

CHAPTER EIGHT

CORA

Footsteps followed me up the stairwell, leaving me in a fizz of anticipation.

I'd been a mess walking home from the club—fine, wobbling my way home—after what we'd done together in the parking lot. And I knew Valentine would rip me a new one because I was lost in my head the entire time, not in the least security conscious, but thinking back over the entire evening, from wishing he was there, to seeing him again. Flirting with him shamelessly until the moment when I told him I was going to dance and read the raw hunger in his eyes and then...

That was it. That was the moment that everything came back to. Probably a whole lot before, tension building between us all week, but tonight, it was *that moment*. When he took my hand and led me through the crowd, his hands landing on my waist as I moved just for him, his eyes drinking me in.

I'd never felt so worshipped in my entire life.

That I'd fallen for the new Chimera's defender was an absolute, unequivocal *yes*. Resounding, and completely unethical, at least from where I stood on my wobbling, exhausted, slicked legs as I pushed my building door open and hauled my trembling body upstairs, praying he wouldn't make me wait too long.

When the footsteps—slow, deliberate and absolutely meant to be heard—echoed mine in the same, slow rhythm, I knew the person making them followed me for a reason.

Valentine hid the sounds of his approach well. I hadn't heard his bike this time at all, hadn't seen his shadow lurking in any of the alleys near my apartment building. Not that my attention had been on such things since I'd been concentrating on...well him. Just the version of him from about an hour ago.

Yes, he could tell me off about that later too, though I didn't think he'd yell. Valentine had his own way of hauling my ass back to reality with a quiet word, or even no words at all.

He certainly hadn't used a lot of those tonight, and the ones he had used were...

Well placed.

That *good girl* still reverberated through me. My face heated for the millionth time as I pushed my key into the lock, blessedly turned it on the fourth try, and managed to open my door. I left the lock off, the door ajar as requested and headed for my room, shedding clothing as I went.

The beaded dress was discarded first, my bag with my other things in it left in the kitchen. My phone vibrated in my bag and I extracted it to find a one word message from my Chimera of choice.

Valentine: RUN, Cora.

I smiled, staring at the screen as I listened for his entry into my apartment, but the hallway remained silent. Anticipation built in my belly. I tapped out a reply.

Cora: The door is open for you. xx

When he didn't reply, I shoved my phone back into my bag that matched my discarded dress and tugged remnants of tape from my boobs. Shaking my head, I fluffed my hair out, deciding to leave my heels on. Valentine seemed like the kind of man who would appreciate a little playacting and drama after all.

A glance over my shoulder told me that I was still the sole occupant of the apartment, though I didn't put it past him to sneak in and watch me undress. It seemed to be the sort of thing he would be into. Maybe we could make a game of it later on, another night.

The stickiness between my thighs reminded me of tonight's game. I headed straight for my bedroom, and climbed onto my bed. My toys were in my top drawer. I left the curtains hanging open; at the height of my top floor building, even though it was older and not in the best of areas, no one was around to look in. Still, I liked being able to see the world in the evenings and I rarely closed the place up.

Lying back on my bed, I scrounged in the drawer with one hand, seeking...*yes*. I came up with hard, cold metal, and snapped one end up the handcuffs around my wrist. The other end I attached to the bed frame, and the key I pressed to the middle of the decorative pillow beside me.

A present for Valentine whenever he decided to release me.

On impulse, I grabbed the next thing I found in the drawer: a silky blindfold that came with a toy pack once that I'd never used. What was the point with no one to watch me, no one to hide myself from? But tonight I had a watcher.

The front door creaked, and snicked softly as it shut. I fumbled the satin black mask over my eyes one handed and lay back, attempting to breathe gently and not hyperventilate. My legs spread a little, then wider. *Why not?* It was his mess on display, and mine, after all. Maybe he'd do us both a favor and clean me up? The thought left me hot and gushing. I moaned softly, tilting my hips restlessly as the footsteps found my room and stopped.

Within seconds I had a love/hate relationship with the blindfold.

I loved that I had to rely on my other senses to form a picture of what was going on in my bedroom around me, but also I hated that I couldn't read Valentine's expression. Was he happy with how I'd presented myself? Did he want something different?

A frustrated noise built in my chest. I slapped the pillow, intent on freeing myself with the key I'd left there and...

Came up empty.

"Oh, Cora. No. That's not going to happen."

I froze at the high pitched, thin voice that most definitely wasn't Valentine's deeper, smoother version.

Why did I leave the door unlocked? Shit. I left it open for any random, to walk on in. But this wasn't just a stranger. This man knew my name, and that little fact made my home invasion, invitation open or not, so much worse.

A spark of recognition as he talked fritzed my brain through my fear of lying bare before someone I swore I knew.

"Key, please," a voice said faintly. After a moment, I figured out it was mine, though I felt like both the voice and my body were a mile away. "Key," I said, my volume a little stronger. "You shouldn't be in my home," I berated the stranger who refused to answer me. "My boyfriend will be here soon, and he'll be...upset."

"No, he won't." The thin voice that I couldn't place held a degree of mirth. "He's still back at the club talking with our friends. But then you knew he wouldn't really come after you, didn't you Cora? Which means that you're really all mine tonight."

I blinked behind the cursed mask, the darkness cloying and thick. Shaking my head, I tipped my body to one side, raising my hand to pull it from my face, but something hard—a forearm or a knee—clamped down on my wrist, pining my arm to the mattress.

"No, Miss Brooks. I don't think so. Not after your little *fuck you* this afternoon, then deciding that you'd flirt with a hockey plater instead of your media kin, yeah?"

I shook my head again, trying to wake up from the twisted fever dream, but I couldn't. Whatever this was, I'd hit reality in a way I couldn't escape. The fear I'd held at bay with dissociation and distance slammed into me at street level. Pain and fear left me choking on a breath I couldn't swallow and when I did, my only thought was to make as much noise as I could.

Warn him.

Drawing my knees to my chest, I sucked in a deep breath. "Valen–" I screamed.

Or half screamed.

Material stuffed into my mouth followed by thin tape that slapped over my face. Tape that had been stuck between my boobs and my beaded dress earlier.

"Fuck," I mumbled through the impromptu gag that I thought might be socks from my drawer. Then the penny dropped. *Hockey player. Media.* "Peatie?"

My words didn't come out like his name, and I only managed to drool on myself.

"So pretty." Fingers swirled at the corners of my lips as I held my breath, then dropped slower. I squeezed my eyes tight, the vulnerability slamming into me for a fraction of a second too late before a mouth touched my skin.

A mouth I didn't want on me and that had no permission to be there. Peatie's hot, wet lips sucked the skin above my breast, then bit down.

I screamed into the sock, but that came out garbled and muffled, too. Tears coated my cheeks, mixing with my saliva. "Stop," I begged as his fingers trailed lower.

"I like to mark my girls up before I ruin them. It's a habit of mine." I shuddered at the realization, curling in on myself, my knees tightened around my stomach, but that left my back bare and exposed. A hand touched the curve of my ass, then the mouth returned. I flinched away, rolling and kicking and shrieking but the tape that had held up so marvelously all night continued to do its job.

Fucking kudos to you.

I screamed again as those hands and mouth found other places to bite, Peatie's light weight settling over me and forcing my legs open.

116

I forgot how to scream after a while and forgot how to fight, thrashing and slapping at air but he was always there. My body ached where he bit me, my head screaming in silence words that refused to exit my mouth as he decorated my skin in marks I feared I'd have to wear forever, and hate myself for every single day.

Bite marks.

Bruises.

Corinne Weathers.

Valentine helping her that night in the club that the media reported on him and the Chimeras. Her refusing to report anything, and only willing to talk to him.

The marks over her body that I could bet my job matched the ones now on mine.

I cried harder and lashed out again, connected a hit with my heel against something solid to my side where I didn't expect it. Something solid that said *oof.*

A different voice.

"Valentine?" I whispered, hope filling my voice. Hope that I prepared to be dashed.

Don't let Peatie have brought his friends. Please, no.

I curled tighter, turning to the side I thought the men weren't in, not that it would stop them.

The touches stopped. And the biting.

"I'm here, Cora. Here for you," Valentine reassured me. His hands swept over my body as I flinched, unable to control the motion, and the blindfold came off.

I stared into dark, rage filled eyes, his control carefully tethered as his arms folded around me. A second later, the metal bracelet at my wrist fell away. I cried out and launched into his chest, burrowing deep.

"It's okay, Cora. It's okay. He can't hurt you again. Not anymore."

"How do you know?" I sniffled at his shirt and tried not to be disgusting, though my tears were anything but the pretty sort.

"Because he had an accident with your stairwell. Apparently he thought he could fly."

I pulled back to stare into Valentine's face and found no evidence of a lie there. Not a truth either.

I clung to him, shivering and trembling. "You know, the last goalie the Chimeras had used to defend the team from everything as well," I said as flashing lights illuminated my apartment from the street level through the open door and the stairwell.

I didn't need to look to know the trust that Valentine didn't say. Maybe I should be scared but... I wasn't. Not anymore.

Bootsteps invaded my home as I clung to Valentine, ignoring the chatter around us. He fielded the questions, thick arms strong and protective around me, a barrier against the world.

"I called the police earlier. Figured out too late where he would be, that you were his next obsession. I hope it mattered." His kiss on my lips was tender and sweet and left me aching and needy for more.

"*Iloveyou*," I mumbled the mangled words into his shirt as a disgruntled, unknown someone told Valentine that they'd have to come back and talk to me later.

We both ignored them.

"Me too," he echoed my garbled words with a clarity I couldn't muster. "I'm in love with you, Cora. There is no one else, not for me," he murmured.

I rested my head on his shoulder, letting him tug a quilt around me. *No one else.* That was a sentiment I could get behind right now. I sighed into the family rhythm of his heartbeat and stole a few more seconds before our peace was blasted to pieces again.

But that's how Valentine and I had always been, it seemed, even in the few days that we'd know each other. Rushing about, trying to make our strange, frantic relationship to work even as we orbited around the other all day. And when we spent time together it was what time allowed, rather than what we planned out.

"Thank you for coming for me. He— Peatie," I forced his name through my lips. "He said you wouldn't," I whispered.

Valentine's arms tightened around me. "And you believed him?" he murmured, his voice soft though his arms remained stiff. Tension rolled off my protector Chimera as I pressed my body to his.

"I thought maybe you were sick of me." The confession stung, even though it was true.

He pressed a kiss to my temple, then a more tender version to my lips that shattered my heart on the spot. "Never going to happen, Cora. I'm in too deep for that to happen."

I smiled at that last. Because funnily enough, so was I.

Despite all the promises I made to myself when I took on the Chimeras this time around, the promises that said I wouldn't get involved with a player, that I wouldn't care and that I wouldn't let a single one of them get under my skin...

I was in too deep, just like him.

EPILOGUE

CORA

We crowded into Coach's office with his present, the three of us, and a chair.

It sounded like the first line of a bad joke, and the space felt like the entire team was jammed into the small area while in reality it was just my tame Chimera who consumed every inch of breathable air and space.

"For you," I presented the new leather office chair officially to the chimeras coach in the wake of the mess that started with Heath Valentine and ended with both of us.

Ward Bishop looked at both of us across his desk

and posed his ass over his worn, used chair. "And if I like this one?" he said, both eyebrows raised as he made to sit.

I opened my mouth to object, horror building in my throat. I knew what I'd done on that chair, and I could *not* be in this room if he sat on it.

Valentine wrapped a firm arm around my midsection, squeezing tightly. "That's your choice. We can donate this one to the hospital, maybe?' he said smoothly. "I'm sure they have some underpaid doctors who need ergonomic support. Coach." He placed a hand on the chair and wheeled it backward a step.

"Stubborn ass," I muttered under my breath.

"What was that?" Ward barked at me, crooking a finger.

I wince and earned a jab in the back for my efforts. "Seriously? Both of you?" I shot Valentine a glare and then turned back to Ward. "That's hardly fair." I towed the chair with me, engaging with tug-of-war with my Chimera of choice.

Valentine relinquished, and I knew I would pay for my brattiness later in some not so subtle way.

Ward waited until I pushed the chair closer and exchanged it for the old one. I clung to the trashed desk chair and passed it safely backward. *Mission accomplished.*

"This one is so much better for your health," I reassured Ward, breathing a little easier.

"I'll bet," Coach muttered, fixing me with a hard stare. His lips twitched, but he didn't say anything else. "Go on. Don't you both have jobs to do?"

"Are you grumpier than usual?" I watched him carefully. Asking Ward Bishop if he was alright was the stupidest thing anyone in the Chimeras club building could do and I knew better. But still...

Valentine gripped my elbow. "Come on butterfly. You got your way."

"Just a minute." I batted his hand away, earning myself a warning squeeze. Whatever. I cared about both men standing in this office with me, for different reasons. "Ward?"

He looked down at the knuckles he rested on his desk, and cleared his throat. "It's my anniversary today."

"Oh?" I blinked at him when he wouldn't look at me. "Did you forget a present? I can lend you my assistant, Liz. She's excellent at gift selection."

Ward jerked his head once. "Sure. Send her in."

Valentine's hand closed on my arm, hauling me out of the office as I called my goodbyes.

I huffed at him. "That was rude."

He tapped my nose and pulled me in closer. "You don't know, do you?"

"What?"

"Coach and his wife. They're estranged. They're both as stubborn as each other and won't break up, but can't stay together. He sees her once a year, apparently."

My mouth dropped open. "What the fuck?" I just found my Chimera. There was no way I was letting him go. "When?"

"Today. Their anniversary."

Thank you for reading Cora and Valentine's story. I hope you loved meeting them! Please leave a review here. If you want to read more Jericho Chimeras, Coach's story is next in PUCK MY WIFE.

ABOUT THE AUTHOR

USA *Today* Bestselling author Sofia Aves writes fast-paced police romances, sizzling military units, steamy cowboys with a Montana backdrop and the occasional cheeky god. Sofia writes kidlit for charity and has over one hundred and fifty publications across six not-so-super-secret pen names. As acquisitions editor for Evernight and Evernight Teen publishing she loves discovering new talent in romance and YA spaces, and is a mum of three crazies in a returned veteran household. Sofia has two overly large fur babies who think they're teacup puppies, a duck who prefers to eat from a dog bowl and two axolotls named after a dragon and a firebird.

Sofia lives near Brisbane, Australia, where she has her own alpaca park, Lorendel.

www.sofiaaves.com

Sign up to <u>Sofia's newsletter</u> and get a free Blue Blooded Brothers book.

Haven't read the Z Boy's prequel? Get it for free here:
A TABLE FOR TEN
Follow Sofia on
BookBub
Twitter
Instagram
<u>Facebook</u>

READ SOFIA'S SERIES

Blue Blooded Brothers
  Collision
  Politics & Paperwork
Blindsided
Sentinel
Mugshots & Candy Canes
Impact
Reckoning
Red Hart Ranch
Snow on the Range
Siren on the Range
Sundown on the Range
Spirit on the Range
Ash on the Range
Mistletoe on the Range

Forgotten Mountain Man
Texan Devils
Ranger's Wish
Ranger Bedevilled
Ranger's Passion
Ranger's Fury
Ranger's Wrath
Ranger's Storm
Snapdragons & Seductions
Summer with a Ranger
Merry with a Ranger
Beach Duty Collection
Playing to Win
Off Boarding
Vicious Slash
Zero Pointer
Off Stage Fling
Rippton Allstars
Crushing It
Glacial Force
Rippton Creatives
Study Games
Make Me, Break Me
Twisted Obsession
Spring Break with a Mafia Prince
A Royally Fake French Menage

Angel Shot
Jericho Chimeras
Puck Me Always
Puck My Heart
Puck me Sideways
Z Boys
King
Joker
Hearts
Ace
Mayhem & Mistletoe
Ruski
Fast Track to Love
Speed Trap
Klauss Brothers
Zander
Keegan
Gallo Empire *with Jade Marshall*
Splintered Vows
Fractured Vows
Fierce Vows
Savage Covenant

Rom Coms
She's A Hot Christmas Mess

Boats, Moats and Root Beer Floats

Writing Romantasy as
SOFIA SHELLEY
Dead Poets Sorority

Writing Reverse Harem Dark Romance as
DOVE PRIEST
Recurve Ridge

Kidlit writing as
JO SEYSENER
The OCD Elf
The OCD Elf's Great Reindeer Calamity
Greg and the Egg

writing YA as
JOSS PHOENIX
Alchem Academy
HIDE FROM US

. . .

Writing spicy paranormal romance as

RAVEN HUSH

Club Fray

Darkest Desires

Purge

Kidnapped By Claws

Ruin

Shadow Lords

Sinner's End

Heaven's Gate (2026)

Monster Brides

Phoenix's Eternal Flame

Kraken's Vow

Krampus' Christmas Bride

Silent Sentinels Duet

Reflections of Silence

Echoes in the Void

Monsters In New York

Feral Moon Rising

Dark Water Refuge